Nancy's added the just-washed straw-berries into the mix. Then she put the top on and hit the BLEND button. The mixture inside quickly became a pinkish-red mush.

*Mmmm!* Nancy thought. *My smoothie is going to be awesome!*

The smoothie continued bubbling . . . and bubbling . . . and bubbling. Nancy stared at it. Her smile froze on her face.

Something was wrong. There were way too many bubbles. In fact the bubbles were pushing against the top of the blender.

A few seconds later the top fell away, and the bubbly mixture came pouring out of the blender and onto the counter.

Nancy gasped. Her smoothie was going out of control!

## The Nancy Drew Notebooks

Available from Simon & Schuster

# THE
# NANCY DREW
# NOTEBOOKS®

#53

*Recipe for Trouble*

## CAROLYN KEENE
ILLUSTRATED BY PAUL CASALE

Aladdin Paperbacks
New York London Toronto Sydney Singapore

First Aladdin Paperbacks edition April 2003

Copyright © 2003 by Simon & Schuster, Inc.

ALADDIN PAPERBACKS
An imprint of Simon & Schuster
Children's Publishing Division
1230 Avenue of the Americas
New York, NY 10020

The text of this book was set in Excelsior.

Printed in the United States of America
10 9 8 7 6 5 4 3

Library of Congress Control Number 2002112592

ISBN 0-689-85680-6

# 1

# A Sweet Spring Vacation

"Yay! It's spring vacation!" Eight-year-old Nancy Drew said happily.

Nancy's best friend George Fayne, whose real name was Georgia, skipped along next to her. "No school for a whole week!" George said.

George's cousin, Bess Marvin, trailed behind the two of them. Bess was Nancy's other best friend. "But what are we going to *do* for a whole week?" Bess moaned. "We'll be totally bored!"

The three girls were walking home from Carl Sandberg Elementary School. They were third-graders there. It was Friday afternoon, the beginning of their spring vacation.

The warm April breeze stirred Nancy's strawberry-blonde hair. There were flowers everywhere: pink cherry blossoms, yellow daffodils, and bright red tulips. Nancy loved spring!

"There's *lots* of stuff we could do for spring vacation," Nancy told Bess.

Bess scrunched her nose. "Really? Like what?"

"We could play video games," George suggested.

"I'm sick of my video games!" Bess complained.

"We could do science experiments," Nancy said.

"That's too much like school," Bess pointed out.

"Don't worry, Bess, we'll come up with a really fun plan!" George told her.

They soon got to Nancy's house. Bess and George had gotten permission to stay for dinner too.

Nancy and her friends found the Drews' housekeeper, Hannah Gruen, in the kitchen.

Hannah had helped Mr. Drew take care of Nancy since Nancy's mother died five years ago. She was flipping through a cookbook.

Nancy's dog, Chocolate Chip, was sitting at Hannah's feet. She was a black Labrador puppy. Chip bounced to her feet and licked Nancy's hand.

"Hi, ladies," Hannah called out cheerfully. "I was just looking for something yummy to make for dinner."

Nancy put her backpack on the counter. She gave Hannah a hug. "How about tacos? Your tacos are super-yummy!"

"How about chocolate cake?" Bess suggested. "Your chocolate cake is super-*super*-yummy!"

Hannah laughed. "Chocolate cake is usually for dessert."

"Did someone say dessert?"

Nancy turned around. Carson Drew was standing in the doorway. He was dressed in a blue suit, white shirt, and a tie with Labrador puppies all over it. Nancy had given the tie to him last year for Father's Day.

Nancy ran up to her father and threw her arms around his neck. "Hi, Daddy!"

"Hi, Pudding Pie," he said. "Pudding Pie" was his special nickname for her. "Hi, Bess. Hi, George. Hi, Hannah. Are you all plotting what to make for dinner?"

"Yes, Daddy!" Nancy replied.

"And *before* that, we were plotting something else—what to do for spring vacation," George piped up.

Bess nodded. "We didn't come up with any cool ideas, though. So we have lots more plotting to do."

Mr. Drew's blue eyes twinkled. "Well, I may be able to help you out with that one."

"You can, Daddy?" Nancy said excitedly.

"I sure can."

Mr. Drew reached into his suit pocket and pulled out a colorful brochure.

Nancy and her friends gathered around him and stared at the brochure.

It said:

Welcome to Le Gourmet Cooking School
Weeklong Dessert-Making Class
For Ages 8–10

Cookies, Cakes, and Other Fun Desserts
Taught by Renowned Chef
Monsieur Jadot!

Underneath the caption was a photograph of a man. He had a big round face, curly black hair, and a bushy black mustache. He wore a tall white chef's hat on his head.

"Cool hat!" George said.

Nancy flipped open the brochure. Inside were photos of desserts—*lots* of desserts. She saw a fancy-looking cake with flowers all over it. There was also a blueberry pie with whipped cream on top, plus there was a plate piled high with brownies and cupcakes.

Bess's blue eyes grew enormous. "Now I'm *really* hungry."

"I still don't get it," Nancy said to her father. "What does this have to do with spring vacation?"

"I called Monsieur Jadot. There are still some openings left in his dessert-making class for kids. And it starts next Monday!" Mr. Drew announced.

"Can I take it, can I take it?" Nancy begged her father.

Mr. Drew nodded. Then he turned to George and Bess.

"I talked to your parents this morning. They said you girls could take the class too, if you want," he said.

Bess and George began jumping up and down. "Yes! Yes!" they said together.

"Will they be making those fancy French desserts, like crème broo-whatchamacallit?" Hannah said worriedly. "Won't that be too difficult for the kids?"

Mr. Drew shook his head. "I think Monsieur Jadot saves the fancy French desserts for the adult class. In the children's class he sticks to cookies and brownies and other basic desserts."

Nancy couldn't believe it. She and her friends were going to spend their spring vacation making desserts!

"Thank you, Daddy!" she said, hugging her father.

"No problem. Now what was that I heard about chocolate cake for dinner?" Mr. Drew asked, grinning.

**\*\*\*\***

"*Bonjour,* ladies and gentlemen! Welcome to my class. I am Monsieur Jadot. That's pronounced 'ja dough,' like cookie dough."

Nancy sat up taller on her kitchen stool so she could see Monsieur Jadot better. He looked just like he did in his picture.

It was the first day of dessert-making class. Nancy looked around. The classroom was a huge kitchen with lots of sinks and stoves. There was a long marble counter with a dozen stools. The air smelled like cinnamon and sugar.

Bess and George were sitting on the stools on either side of Nancy. Bess was wearing a pink apron with ruffles all over it. George was dressed how she was usually dressed: jeans and a soccer jersey.

There were five other kids in the class. Nancy knew some of them from school. There was Brenda Carlton, who was kind of snobby and mean, and her friend Alison Wegman. Kenny Bruder, who was in fourth grade, was also taking the class.

Nancy didn't recognize the other two kids. Their nametags read: MIDORI TANAKA

and JARED STEIN. Midori had long, shiny black hair, and brown eyes. Jared had curly red hair, and glasses. They looked like they were the same age as Nancy and her friends.

*They must go to River Heights Elementary School,* Nancy thought.

"And speaking of cookie dough!" Monsieur Jadot exclaimed. "We are going to spend the week making cookies and other excellent desserts. You will become young dessert experts!"

Kenny Bruder raised his hand. "Do we get to eat them, too?"

"*Mais, oui.* Of course!" Monsieur Jadot said.

"What does he mean, 'may we'?" Bess whispered to Nancy.

"I think that's French for 'of course,'" Nancy whispered back.

"At the end of the week, your papas and mamas will be invited to a special party," Monsieur Jadot continued. "They will taste your dessert creations. Also at the party I will award a prize for Top Chef. The winner will receive a most beautiful trophy as well as a very special dessert created by me, Monsieur Jadot."

"What is it, what is it?" Bess burst out.

"It is my very own strawberry mousse cake," Monsieur Jadot replied, twirling his mustache.

"Yum!" Bess said.

"Double-yum!" George agreed.

"I'm going to work extra-hard to try to win the prize," Nancy told Bess and George.

"Yes, of course you will!" Monsieur Jadot exclaimed, overhearing Nancy. "I assure you my strawberry mousse cake will be worth it!" He turned to the blackboard.

Just then, Nancy felt something hit her on the side of the head. A paper airplane landed on the counter in front of her.

Nancy was annoyed but curious. She opened the airplane.

Inside was a message scribbled in blue Magic Marker. It said: There's no way you're going to be Top Chef because I will!

# 2

# The Cupcake Disaster

Nancy couldn't believe it. Who would be mean enough to send a paper airplane crashing into her head—especially one with a nasty message on it?

Nancy glanced around the room. She did a double take.

Kenny Bruder was staring at her. When Nancy caught his eye he blushed and turned away.

Then Nancy noticed that he had blue Magic Marker smudged on his right hand.

"Kenny Bruder, *you* did that!" Nancy blurted out. She heard Brenda and Alison snickering.

Monsieur Jadot stopped writing on the blackboard and whirled around. "What is happening?" he demanded.

Nancy pointed at Kenny. "He threw a paper airplane at me!" she told Monsieur Jadot.

"Did not!" Kenny shot back. He blushed even more.

Monsieur Jadot marched over to Nancy's stool. He picked up the piece of paper and read the message on it.

Then he marched over to Kenny's stool. He frowned at the blue smudges on Kenny's right hand.

"I'm afraid you are—how do you say it—busted," Monsieur Jadot told Kenny sternly. "The evidence is all over your hand. Monsieur Bruder, in the future, please refrain from these foolish shenanigans. I do not tolerate flying objects in my room."

"Yes, sir," Kenny mumbled. He slouched down on his stool.

George leaned over to Nancy. "Why is Kenny being such a bully?" she whispered.

Nancy shrugged. "I don't know. But I'm just going to ignore him."

"Definitely," Bess agreed. "Let's *all* ignore him. We'll just make yummy desserts and have fun!"

Monsieur Jadot returned to the blackboard and continued scribbling. "Flour . . . egg . . . sugar," he read out loud. "These are some of the ingredients that will go into today's recipe."

"What *is* today's recipe, Monsieur Jadot?" Midori Tanaka asked.

"*Les petits gâteaux,*" Monsieur Jadot announced. "That is to say, cupcakes!"

Nancy noticed Jared Stein lean over and say something to Midori. Midori smiled. *They must be friends,* Nancy thought.

"Cupcakes!" Bess cried out. "Yay! They're my favorite dessert."

Monsieur Jadot looked around the kitchen. "We need to pass out aprons and chef's hats. But where is my assistant?" He frowned.

Just then the door burst open. A girl came running into the kitchen. She had long, curly red hair that was tied back into a ponytail. She was wearing jeans and a wrinkly white T-shirt that read CHOCOLATE FREAK on the back. She looked

like she was about fourteen years old.

"Where have you been, Annabelle?" Monsieur Jadot said, putting his hands on his hips. "You were supposed to be here thirty minutes ago!"

"I'm sorry, Papa. I was helping out in the office and I forgot the time," Annabelle said breathlessly.

"I need you to pass out aprons and hats. Oh, and please lay out all the ingredients for this assignment," Monsieur Jadot said.

"Okay, Papa," Annabelle said. Under her breath she added, "Whatever." Monsieur Jadot didn't hear her, but Nancy did.

"Monsieur Jadot's assistant is his daughter!" Nancy whispered to her friends.

"It's funny that she works for her dad," George remarked.

"Have *you* ever worked for your dad, Nancy?" Bess asked.

"Not really. But maybe someday I will. I could help him with his cases," Nancy said with a grin.

Carson Drew was a lawyer. He often handled tough cases where he had to solve a mystery or two.

Nancy *loved* solving mysteries. She had already solved a bunch of mysteries at school and elsewhere. In fact her father had given her a special blue notebook for keeping track of suspects and clues.

Annabelle passed white chef's hats and white aprons to the eight students in the class. Bess took off her pink ruffly apron and put on one of the white ones, so she, Nancy, and George would match.

Soon all eight kids were wearing the chef's hats and aprons. *We look like real chefs in a fancy restaurant!* Nancy thought.

"*Mademoiselles et monsieurs,* let me explain to you all about the art of the cupcake," Monsieur Jadot said. He held up two mixing bowls, one in each hand. "It is basically like making a cake. In one bowl we will mix the dry ingredients: flour, baking powder, salt. In another bowl we will mix the wet ingredients: butter, then sugar, then egg yolks."

"But sugar isn't wet," Brenda pointed out. She flipped her long, dark hair over her shoulders.

"Yes, but it will be after it is mixed with the butter and eggs," Monsieur Jadot explained.

Soon the room was filled with the sounds of eggs cracking and beaters whirring. Monsieur Jadot and Annabelle carefully supervised while the students used the beaters.

Nancy had made cupcakes before, with Hannah and her father. But these cupcakes seemed extra-special. Maybe it was because she was making them in a real cooking school!

"I'm going to decorate my cupcakes with flowers," Bess said as she licked butter from her fingers.

"That's dumb! I'm going to decorate *my* cupcakes with the flags of countries in Europe!" Brenda bragged.

"Miss Show-off!" Bess muttered under her breath.

Monsieur Jadot went around the room and showed everyone how to pour their cupcake batter into muffin tins.

An hour later everyone's cupcakes were

done. The room was filled with wonderful baking smells. Monsieur Jadot and Annabelle helped everyone take their cupcakes out of the oven.

Nancy was really proud of her cupcakes. They had come out golden-brown, and she had decorated them with yummy chocolate frosting and silver sprinkles.

"I will now sample everyone's creations," Monsieur Jadot announced.

"Ohhh, I hope he likes mine!" George whispered to Nancy and Bess.

Monsieur Jadot went to Jared's workstation first. He picked up one of Jared's cupcakes and took a large bite. "Very good . . . ah, *très bien!* You have talent, Monsieur Stein."

"Gosh, thanks." Jared adjusted his glasses and broke into a big smile.

Next Monsieur Jadot tasted one of Brenda's cupcakes. "Ah, excellent! You too have talent, Mademoiselle Carlton!"

"Thank you," Brenda said to Monsieur Jadot. Then she turned to Nancy and her friends and gave them a smug smile.

After Brenda, Monsieur Jadot came over

to George's workstation. Nancy knew that George had worked extra-hard on her cupcakes. Each one was decorated with strawberry frosting and thin little strawberry slices.

Monsieur Jadot lifted one of George's cupcakes to his mouth. He took a big bite—and made a horrible face. He spit the cupcake out.

"*Bleh!* This is awful!" Monsieur Jadot cried out. "This is the worst cupcake I have ever tasted in my life!"

# 3

# Bubble Trouble

Monsieur Jadot grabbed a bottle of sparkling water from the counter and gulped down half of it. "Ugh! *C'est terrible!* Mademoiselle Fayne, what on Earth did you put in your so-called cupcakes?" he practically yelled at George.

George's eyes swam with tears. "I-I just put in what you said, Monsieur Jadot. S-Sugar and flour and eggs and stuff like that. P-Plus my special strawberry frosting," she added, her lips quivering.

"Strawberry frosting! This does not taste like strawberry frosting. This tastes more like . . . like . . . mouthwash!" Monsieur Jadot took another gulp of the sparkling water.

"Don't worry, George. Maybe he's just in a crabby mood," Bess whispered to her cousin.

"Yeah, he's in a crabby mood—about my cupcake!" George said, sniffling. "Jared's cupcake didn't make him crabby. Neither did Brenda's!"

Across the room, Brenda whispered something to Alison. The two girls started giggling.

Nancy peered over at George's plate. Nancy picked up one of George's cupcakes. She looked at it carefully.

She noticed that the pink frosting was sparkly. *That's weird,* she thought. *Why would strawberry frosting be sparkly?*

Then Nancy brought the cupcake up to her nose and sniffed. It smelled minty.

She stuck her pinkie finger in the frosting, then took a lick. She made a face. It was toothpaste!

"Yuck!" Nancy cried out.

George looked hurt. "Oh, no, Nancy! Now you're crabby about my cupcake too!"

Nancy shook her head quickly. "No,

George, that's not it! There's toothpaste in this frosting!"

"Toothpaste!" George repeated. "No way!"

"What else did you put in there, Fayne? Dental floss?" Kenny guffawed. Brenda and Alison began cracking up.

"It's definitely toothpaste," Nancy said worriedly. "How did it get there?"

"I didn't put it there," George insisted.

"Well, if you didn't, who did?" Bess piped up.

Monsieur Jadot put his bottle of sparkling water down with a loud thump. "Toothpaste? But how could this be?" he cried out.

He turned to his daughter, who was taking some cupcakes out of the oven. "Annabelle! Did you double-check all the ingredients for the cupcakes?" he asked her.

"Of course, Papa," Annabelle replied. "I was very careful. Besides, how could I mistake toothpaste for frosting?" She rolled her eyes in exasperation.

"Hmmm," Monsieur Jadot said in a grumpy voice. "I will investigate this situation myself." He frowned at Nancy and the other students. "In the meantime let us continue with our class. I will resume my cupcake inspection. And I'd better not taste any more toothpaste!"

"How did that toothpaste get in my frosting?" George said miserably.

It was around four o'clock in the afternoon. Hannah had picked up the girls at Le Gourmet Cooking School and brought them to the park. The girls were swinging on the swings. Hannah was sitting underneath the shade of a nearby tree. She was reading a cookbook of French cuisine.

"You're sure you didn't accidentally put toothpaste on your cupcakes, by mistake?" Bess asked her cousin. "Did you have a tube of toothpaste in your backpack or something?"

"No way!" George replied.

Nancy leaned back and pumped her legs. Her swing rose higher and higher in the air. She liked the feeling of the wind whipping through her hair.

"That means somebody *put* the toothpaste on your cupcakes," Nancy called out to George.

"I bet Kenny Bruder did it!" Bess exclaimed. "He thinks he is so funny!"

"Or it could have been bratty Brenda," George pointed out.

Hannah came by. "Time to go, girls! I have to get back home and start making dinner. I found a wonderful recipe in here!" She held up the French cookbook.

"What is it, Hannah?" Nancy asked her eagerly. She dug her feet into the dirt to stop her swing. Bess and George did the same.

"Escargot," Hannah replied. "I hope I'm pronouncing that right. My high-school French is a little rusty!"

"Es-car-go? What's that?" Nancy asked her.

"Snails baked in garlic butter," Hannah replied.

Nancy, Bess, and George stared at each other. "Ewwwww!" they all cried out at the same time.

During Tuesday's dessert-making class, Nancy bumped into Midori at the sink.

25

Nancy almost dropped the bowl of strawberries she was carrying.

"Sorry!" Midori cried out.

"Sorry!" Nancy said at the same time.

Midori's cheeks turned bright pink. She looked uncomfortable.

*She seems kind of shy,* Nancy thought.

"What kind of smoothie are you making?" Nancy asked Midori. Today's recipe was for smoothies.

"Ohhhh. I still haven't decided. Maybe a mango-lime smoothie. But maybe that would taste really yucky, I don't know." Midori shrugged.

"A mango-lime smoothie? That sounds yummy!" Nancy said eagerly. "I'm making a strawberry-pineapple smoothie."

"That sounds *really* yummy," Midori told her. "Way yummier than mine."

Midori said good-bye and returned to her workstation. Nancy washed some strawberries in the sink, then headed in the direction of her workstation.

On the way she passed one of the small storage closets. She overheard a voice coming from inside. Surprised, she stopped to listen.

"He is *so* bossy, Alexis. I hate this job! I wish I was working at the Burger Barn with you."

Nancy peeked through the door. Annabelle was sitting on a cardboard box. She was twirling a lock of her long red hair and talking quietly into a purple cell phone. She didn't notice Nancy.

Annabelle went on talking. "But he's getting what he deserves! Wait'll you hear what . . ."

"Annabelle! Where *are* you?"

Nancy glanced around. Monsieur Jadot was looking around and calling for his daughter. She clutched her bowl of strawberries to her chest and kept on walking.

A second later, Annabelle came rushing out of the closet with an armful of supplies. "Coming, Papa!" she exclaimed. The purple cell phone was sticking out of her jeans' pocket.

*What was that all about?* Nancy wondered.

Nancy returned to her workstation. George

and Bess had all their smoothie ingredients packed into their blenders.

"What took you so long?" George asked Nancy.

"I'll tell you later!" Nancy replied.

Soon the entire kitchen was filled with the sound of whirring blenders. Monsieur Jadot and Annabelle showed everyone how to use the blenders properly.

Nancy's blender already had pineapple chunks, pineapple juice, and vanilla yogurt in it. She added the just-washed strawberries into the mix. Then she put the top on and hit the BLEND button.

The blender whirred to life. The fruit, yogurt, and juice mixture inside quickly became a pinkish-red mush.

*Mmmm!* Nancy thought. *My smoothie is going to be awesome!*

The smoothie continued bubbling . . . and bubbling . . . and bubbling. Nancy stared at it. Her smile froze on her face.

Something was wrong. There were way too many bubbles. In fact the bubbles were pushing against the top of the blender.

A few seconds later the top fell away, and the bubbly mixture came pouring out of the blender and onto the counter.

Nancy gasped. Her smoothie was going out of control!

# 4

# A Salty Surprise

Nancy clapped her hand over her mouth. Her smoothie was bubbling out of the blender and onto the counter. It was even spilling onto the floor!

It looked like an erupting volcano!

"What is going on here?"

Nancy turned around. Monsieur Jadot was standing there, his hands on his hips. He looked mad.

"I . . . that is . . . my smoothie exploded!" Nancy sputtered. She could feel her face turning red.

Monsieur Jadot reached over and pushed the OFF button on Nancy's blender. "Mademoiselle Drew, the top is supposed to be *on*, not *off*," he scolded her.

"It *was* on," Nancy explained. "The bubbles made the top fall off."

Some of the other kids gathered around Nancy's blender and stared at the mess. There was strawberry-pineapple smoothie everywhere. It was a disaster!

"What did you put in there? Bubble bath?" Brenda teased.

"Yeah!" Kenny snickered. "Yesterday, George put toothpaste on her cupcakes. Today, Nancy put bubble bath in her smoothie. Maybe tomorrow, Bess will put hair gel in her Jell-O!"

"That's enough, Monsieur Bruder and Mademoiselle Carlton," Monsieur Jadot snapped. "In the meantime I don't want anyone tasting any of their smoothies until I've investigated this situation." He began inspecting everyone's smoothies.

"Why did your smoothie go crazy like that?" Bess asked Nancy.

"I'm not sure," Nancy replied worriedly. "I followed the recipe exactly. I don't know what happened!"

Then Nancy noticed something strange. Behind her blender, a red box was peeking out from under a stained white dishtowel.

Nancy pulled the box out from underneath the dishtowel. The front of the box read: BAKING SODA.

"Baking soda?" Nancy said out loud. "What's *that* doing there? I didn't put baking soda in my smoothie!"

George put her hand on Nancy's arm. "Nancy, remember that experiment in science class?"

Nancy frowned. "Huh?"

"A couple of months ago in science class we made volcanoes out of papier-mâché," George reminded her.

Nancy nodded. "Oh, yeah! And we made them erupt with baking soda and dishwashing detergent!"

"Exactly!" George said.

"Maybe someone put baking soda and detergent in my blender to make my smoothie erupt—like a volcano!" Nancy said angrily. She glanced around the kitchen. "And I'm going to find out who!"

Right after class that day Nancy, George, and Bess headed over to Nancy's house.

As soon as they got there they rushed upstairs to Nancy's room and flopped down on the bed. Then Nancy pulled her detective notebook out of her backpack.

"Do you girls need snacks, or are you all too filled up on fancy desserts?" Hannah called from downstairs.

"Snacks, please!" all three girls shouted.

Nancy flipped through her blue notebook until she found a clean page. She reached into her backpack and found her favorite purple pen.

Across the top of the page, she wrote, "The Case of the Messed-up Recipes."

"Okay," Nancy said to George. "Someone in our class messed up your recipe and my recipe. The question is who?"

"And why?" George added.

"I think it's Kenny Bruder," Bess said. She twirled a lock of her blond hair around and around on her finger. "He sent you that nasty airplane message, remember? He really

wants to win the Top Chef prize. Maybe he's messing up other kids' recipes so he'll win for sure!"

"He's definitely a suspect," Nancy agreed. She wrote:

> Suspects:
> Kenny Bruder
> He really wants to win
> the Top Chef prize!

Then Nancy remembered Annabelle's cell-phone conversation. She told Bess and George about it.

"Maybe *Annabelle*'s the kitchen bandit," George said when Nancy had finished.

"No way! She's super-cool. Besides, she wears really cute clothes!" Bess protested.

George giggled. "So what? Monsieur Jadot is really bossy with her. Maybe Annabelle's trying to ruin his class to make him mad!"

"Hmm. You could be right," Nancy said.

Under Kenny Bruder's name in the Suspects column, Nancy wrote:

Annabelle Jadot
Her dad is super-bossy.
Maybe she wants to get even!

Just then, Hannah came through the door. She was carrying a tray.

Bess craned her neck to see what was on the tray. "Mmm, chocolate-chip cookies! And lemonade!" she said eagerly.

"Maybe we should check to make sure there isn't any toothpaste or something in the cookies," George joked.

Hannah looked confused. "Toothpaste? In *my* cookies?"

Nancy told Hannah about the cupcake incident and the smoothie incident. When she had finished, Hannah said, "Oh, my! That's a real mystery, isn't it?"

Bess nodded. "Yes. But that's okay because Nancy is the best detective in the whole wide world. She's going to solve the mystery!"

Wednesday's class assignment was butterscotch brownies. Because of what had happened on Monday and Tuesday, everyone was very careful with their brownies.

"Stay away from my bowl!" Nancy heard Alison say to Kenny. Alison grabbed her bowl of brownie batter and hugged it tightly.

Kenny glared at her. "I wouldn't go near that if you paid me. It looks gross!" he shot back.

"Please, children, enough!" Monsieur Jadot snapped his fingers. "We cannot become great dessert chefs if we are playing silly games and pranks."

Nancy listened to Monsieur Jadot. She mixed flour into a bowl, then baking powder, then baking soda.

Seeing the red box of baking soda made her think about what had happened yesterday. Who put baking soda and detergent in her smoothie? Was it Kenny? Or Annabelle? Or someone else altogether?

"Are you done with that sugar jar or what?" Brenda snapped at Nancy.

"Here, use this one," Jared said, passing his sugar jar over to Brenda. "I'm done with it."

"Hey, *I* was waiting for that," Kenny said. He intercepted the jar from Jared.

Kenny dumped a ton of sugar into his bowl without measuring it. Then he passed the sugar jar to Brenda. "Here, you can have it now."

"Gee, thanks," Brenda said in a sarcastic voice.

An hour later, everyone's butterscotch brownies were done. Monsieur Jadot and Annabelle helped the students take their brownies out of the oven.

Nancy tasted a sample of hers. It was still warm from the oven. It was yummy, too!

"These are awesome," Bess said, popping a butterscotch brownie into her mouth.

"Mine are too," George agreed, munching on one of hers.

Just then, Brenda let out a shriek. Nancy looked up, startled. "What's the matter, Brenda?" she asked her.

Monsieur Jadot rushed across the kitchen. "*Now* what, Mademoiselle Carlton?" he demanded.

"Someone put tons of *salt* in my brownies!" Brenda screeched.

Alison began making a choking sound. "Mine too!" she cried out.

# 5

# The Chocolate-
# Fingerprint Clue

Nancy was speechless. The kitchen bandit
had struck again! Someone had put salt in
Brenda and Alison's butterscotch brownies!

Then Jared and Kenny started making
gagging noises. "S-S-S-Salt!" Jared sputtered, pointing to his brownies.

"Mine too," Kenny said, pointing to his.
"These are totally gross!"

Monsieur Jadot frowned. He looked really
confused. "What is this? What is going on?"

He picked up one of Brenda's butterscotch brownies and took a small bite. He
spit it out. "*Bleh!* You are right, mademoiselle. Salt! Perhaps you confused the

recipe and put in salt instead of sugar?"

Brenda gaped at Monsieur Jadot. "No way! I followed the recipe exactly," she huffed.

"So did I," Alison insisted.

"Me too," Jared said.

"Me three. I mean, me four," Kenny piped up.

"Hmmm," Monsieur Jadot muttered.

Monsieur Jadot went around and sampled everyone's butterscotch brownies. After he was done, he said, "Four batches are fine: Mademoiselle Drew, Mademoiselle Fayne, Mademoiselle Marvin, and Mademoiselle Tanaka's. The other four batches are *not* fine: Mademoiselle Carlton, Mademoiselle Wegman, Monsieur Stein, and Monsieur Bruder's. This is most mysterious!"

Bess turned to Nancy. "What does that mean?" she whispered. "*Our* brownies were okay, and Midori's, too. But Brenda, Alison, Jared, and Kenny's brownies were *not* okay."

Nancy thought long and hard. What *could* it mean? The guilty person, whoever it was, ruined four batches of brownies. But he or she had left the other four batches alone.

And then Nancy thought of when Monsieur Jadot just said to Brenda about mixing up the sugar with the salt.

"Where's the sugar jar?" Nancy said suddenly to Bess and George.

"You mean the one we used?" George asked her. She glanced around, then pointed to Midori's workstation. "There! It's the jar with the red lid. It says 'sugar' on it. Midori used it after the three of us did."

Nancy rushed over to Midori's workstation.

Midori was sitting on her stool, looking anxious. "Hi, Midori," Nancy said.

"Uh, hi," Midori replied. "What do you want?"

Nancy pointed to the sugar jar. "I just need to check this out," she said.

Nancy twisted the lid off the sugar jar and sniffed. She put her pinkie finger in the sugar and tasted it. It was definitely sugar!

Then Nancy remembered that there was another sugar jar that some of the other

kids had been using. It had a *blue* lid and had the word "sugar" on it.

She glanced around the room. The jar was sitting on the counter at Alison's workstation.

"Thanks, Midori," Nancy said breathlessly. She rushed over to Alison's workstation.

"What are you doing?" Brenda snapped when Nancy picked up the blue-lidded jar.

"I'm just checking something out," Nancy explained. She opened the jar and tasted the sugar with her other pinkie.

Except it wasn't sugar—it was salt!

Nancy took the jar over to Monsieur Jadot and Annabelle. "Monsieur Jadot!" Nancy said excitedly. "I figured it out. Someone put salt in this sugar jar."

*"Impossible!"* Monsieur Jadot cried out. He pronounced it like "am-po-see-blur." He tasted what was in the blue-lidded jar. *"Oui,* you are correct, Mademoiselle Drew. It *is* salt!" he said, looking shocked.

Then he narrowed his eyes and turned to his daughter. "Did you put salt in the sugar jar, Annabelle?"

Annabelle's jaw dropped. "No way! I did *not* do that. I remember putting sugar in both those jars." She looked really annoyed.

Nancy glanced around the room. Kenny snitched a butterscotch brownie from Bess's pan and popped it into his mouth. When he saw Nancy looking at him, he stopped chewing and turned away.

Nancy frowned. Kenny was one of the four kids whose butterscotch brownies had gotten messed up. He was also on her suspect list.

But now Nancy wasn't so sure. Would Kenny have ruined his own brownies?

"Kenny could have put salt in his brownies to keep people from suspecting him," Bess suggested the next day as she, George, and Nancy walked to the Le Gourmet Cooking School.

It was a cloudy day. Next to the sidewalk, a row of yellow daffodils swayed and bobbed in the wind. It looked like it might start raining any second. Nancy was glad she had worn her special blue rain boots and blue raincoat.

"*I* still think it's Annabelle," George piped up. "I forgot to tell you guys. Yesterday, just after class was over, I saw her putting a container of salt in the cupboard!"

"So?" Nancy said.

"So maybe that was the box of salt she dumped into the sugar jar!" George said eagerly.

Nancy nodded. "Hmm. Maybe."

Bess kicked a pebble on the sidewalk. "Hey! Did you guys remember to bring in your favorite dessert recipe?" she asked Nancy and George.

Today was Bring Your Favorite Dessert Recipe day. It was also the second-to-last day of class.

Nancy nodded. "Yes. I brought Hannah's recipe for hot-fudge sundaes."

"I brought my dad's recipe for blueberry crisp," George said.

"I brought my grandma's peanut butter-cookie recipe," Bess said.

The girls continued buzzing excitedly about their recipes until they reached the cooking school. They ran into Brenda at the front door.

"Hi, Brenda," Nancy called out.

Brenda flipped her hair over her shoulders. "Hi, guys. Well I guess you should start congratulating me."

George frowned. "Why?"

"Because I brought in my aunt Maria's extra-special chocolate-fudge recipe. It's going to help me win the Top Chef contest!" Brenda bragged.

"Oh, yeah, right," Bess said. She rolled her eyes.

The other four kids were already in the kitchen when Nancy, Bess, George, and Brenda walked in. Some of them had already started working on their recipes.

Jared was blending something in a blender. "My super-duper extra-fantastic triple-chocolate smoothie!" he announced to Nancy when she said hi to him. He adjusted his glasses. "What are you going to make?"

"A hot-fudge sundae," Nancy told him. "Bess is making peanut-butter cookies, and George is making a blueberry crisp."

"Wow, I guess I have competition," Jared joked.

"Jared always wins everything. He won the science fair at our school last month," Midori piped up. "And last year he won the spelling bee."

"You win stuff too, Midori," Jared said to her. "You came in second at the science fair. And you came in third in the art contest."

"Fifth," Midori said. She sounded kind of glum.

Monsieur Jadot went up to the front of the room and clapped his hands loudly. "Ladies and gentlemen! Today is Bring Your Favorite Dessert Recipe Day. Annabelle and I will help you gather the ingredients you need to make your recipes. Let us get started!"

"I hope no one's going to dump salt into my apple pie!" Nancy heard Alison say to Brenda.

The class got busy making their desserts. Monsieur Jadot and Annabelle supervised.

As Nancy stirred hot-fudge sauce on the stove, she looked around the kitchen. Everything *seemed* okay. Nobody was complaining about weird things happening to their recipes.

Then Nancy felt a tap on her shoulder. She turned around. Bess was standing there. She looked worried.

"What is it, Bess?" Nancy asked her.

"Have you seen the second page of my recipe?" Bess asked her. "It's missing!"

Nancy set her chocolate-covered wooden spoon down. "Huh? What are you talking about?"

"My grandma's recipe for peanut-butter cookies! She wrote it down on two pieces of paper. The second page is missing, and I can't make the cookies without it!" Bess moaned.

"Did you leave it at home?" Nancy asked her.

Bess shook her head. "No! It was on the counter a minute ago. Now it's gone!"

Nancy turned the burner off from underneath her hot-fudge sauce. She walked over to Bess's workstation.

The first page of the recipe was sitting right there. It was next to a jar of peanut butter and a bright red bowl with flour in it. The recipe was written on yellow legal paper with lines on it.

Then Nancy noticed something. Near the piece of paper were smudgy chocolate fingerprints.

"Did you put those there, Bess?" Nancy asked her friend.

Bess shook her head. "Uh-uh."

"George?" Nancy asked her other friend. George was busy making her blueberry crisp.

"Nope. There's no chocolate in my recipe," George replied.

Nancy knew they weren't her fingerprints either. That must mean that whoever stole the second page of Bess's recipe must have left the chocolate fingerprints there!

"Follow me," Nancy whispered to Bess. "Don't say anything to anyone. We'll find out who is making chocolate desserts. One of them has to be the recipe thief!" she said.

The first person Nancy ran into was Alison. Alison was making apple pie. Her workstation smelled like cinnamon and butter.

*She's not the one,* Nancy reasoned.

Kenny's workstation was next to Alison.

Kenny was busy mixing something in a bowl.

Nancy was about to ask Kenny what he was making when she noticed something on the floor.

It was Kenny's backpack. Sticking out of one of the pockets was a piece of yellow paper with lines on it. It had chocolate smudges all over it!

*Kenny's the thief!* Nancy thought.

# 6

## More Suspects in the Mix

Nancy couldn't believe it. She'd caught Kenny red-handed.

*He* was the recipe thief. The evidence was right there in his backpack. And the chocolate fingerprints were even more proof.

Did that mean Kenny put the toothpaste on George's cupcakes, the baking soda and detergent in Nancy's smoothie, and the salt in the sugar jar?

Before Nancy had a chance to say anything, Bess spoke up. "Hey! Kenny Bruder! You stole my grandma's recipe!" she exclaimed.

Kenny turned around. He had flour all over his T-shirt. "Huh? What are you talking about, Bess?"

Bess whipped the piece of yellow paper out of Kenny's backpack. "This! You stole it so I would mess up my cookies and *you* could be Top Chef!" she accused. "That is so totally mean!"

Kenny frowned. "Huh? I don't know how that piece of paper got there. *I* didn't put it there."

"Oh, so it just happened to be in your backpack? By magic?" Bess shot back.

Kenny shrugged. "I don't know. Whatever."

Nancy was about to speak up when she noticed something strange. Kenny didn't have chocolate smudges on his hands.

*So how did the chocolate fingerprints get on the recipe and on the counter?* she wondered.

Nancy also noticed that Kenny wasn't making a chocolate dessert. "What's that?" she asked Kenny, pointing to his mixing bowl.

"Huh? Lemon-cookie batter," Kenny replied. "Can I go back to cooking now?

Or are you two going to arrest me?" He snickered.

Nancy grabbed Bess's arm. "Come on, Bess, let's go."

"But Kenny's the thief!" Bess hissed.

Nancy shook her head. "I'm not sure anymore. It might be somebody else."


"I still think it's Kenny," Bess insisted.

She, Nancy, and George were sitting in a booth at the Double Dip. The Double Dip was their favorite ice cream parlor in town.

Nancy took a bite of her strawberry ice-cream cone. This was her idea of a great spring vacation: eating desserts all day in class, then eating *more* desserts after class!

"But where did those chocolate fingerprints come from, then?" Nancy said. "Kenny wasn't making anything chocolatey."

"Maybe he ate something chocolatey, then later washed his hands," Bess suggested.

George's eyes lit up. "Hey! Brenda made fudge. Maybe she stole your recipe, Bess!"

Bess nodded. "I guess that's true. She could have put the recipe in Kenny's backpack to make him look guilty."

Nancy reached into her backpack and took out her blue notebook and purple pen. "I'm going to have to write all this down," she said.

She quickly found the page that said "The Case of the Messed-up Recipes" across the top of it. Under Suspects, she added:

Brenda Carlton
She made fudge today. Plus she really wants to win the Top Chef contest.

Nancy glanced up from her notebook. "Tomorrow's the last day of class," she reminded her friends. "Our parents will be there for the special dessert party. And Monsieur Jadot will announce the winner of the contest."

"We've gotta solve the mystery by then!" Bess said worriedly. "If we don't, Kenny or Brenda or whoever it is might try to ruin the party!"

"We have three suspects now," Nancy said. She trailed her finger down the open pages in her notebook. "Kenny, Annabelle, and Brenda. We also have a bunch of clues:

the sparkly pink toothpaste, the box of baking soda, and the chocolate fingerprints."

"Hi, Nancy. Hi, Bess. Hi, George."

The girls looked up. Midori had just walked into the Double Dip. She was waving at them with a shy smile.

There was a tall, slender woman with her. She looked a lot like Midori.

The woman and Midori came over to the girls' table.

"Nancy, George, Bess, this is my mom," Midori said. "Mom, these girls are in my dessert-making class."

"Oh, how wonderful!" Mrs. Tanaka gushed. "Midori has told me so much about this class. Her father and I can't wait to come tomorrow and taste all the desserts you've been making."

Nancy was about to say something. But then she noticed a shopping bag hanging on Midori's arm.

The shopping bag was from McPherson's Drug Store in downtown River Heights. It was clear plastic, so Nancy could see right through it.

Inside the bag were two things: a bottle of pink strawberry shampoo and a tube of strawberry-flavored Sparkly Smile toothpaste.

Nancy's heart started to beat faster. The toothpaste on George's cupcakes had been pink and sparkly.

Did Midori put the toothpaste on George's cupcakes? Was *she* the guilty one?

# 7

# Setting a Tasty Trap

Nancy stared and stared at the sparkly pink toothpaste in Midori's shopping bag. Did Midori put toothpaste on George's cupcakes? Did she also put the baking soda and detergent in Nancy's smoothie, dump salt in the sugar jar, and steal the second page of Bess's recipe?

Mrs. Tanaka was talking to Bess, George, and Midori about tomorrow's special dessert party. Nancy had a plan.

"Hey," Nancy interrupted. "That's my favorite kind of toothpaste, Midori!" She pointed to Midori's shopping bag.

Midori looked confused. "What? Oh. It's

my favorite too. I get it all the time."

"Kids' toothpaste flavors! They're practically like desserts, aren't they?" Mrs. Tanaka said, chuckling. "Strawberry, banana, raspberry . . ."

*Midori didn't act nervous when I asked her about the toothpaste,* Nancy thought. She decided to try another approach. "So, Midori! Do you think you'll win the Top Chef contest?"

"Huh? Oh, I don't know," Midori said, shrugging. "Maybe. But I'm not good with desserts like you guys and Jared, you know?"

"Jared, Jared, Jared," Mrs. Tanaka said. She put her arm around her daughter's shoulders. "Jared Stein is Midori's best friend. She looks up to him like a big brother."

"Stop it, Mom," Midori said. A deep blush crept into her cheeks.

A waitress came over and told Mrs. Tanaka and Midori that there was a table ready for them. Mrs. Tanaka and Midori bid the three girls good-bye.

"See you at the party tomorrow!" Mrs. Tanaka said, waving.

Nancy waited until the two of them were all the way across the crowded room. Then she leaned across the table.

"Midori had pink Sparkly Smile toothpaste in her bag!" she whispered. "We have to add her to the suspect list!"

"Midori? She's nice. She wouldn't do all that bad stuff," Bess said, glancing over her shoulder.

"Maybe, maybe not. We still have to add her to the suspect list. Remember, we have to solve this mystery by tomorrow!" Nancy reminded her friends.

Nancy picked up her purple pen and added Midori Tanaka to the suspect list.

Friday was a rainy day. Raindrops splashed against the windows of Monsieur Jadot's kitchen. Nancy, George, Bess, and the other five kids worked to get ready for the special dessert party. They were all baking different kinds of cookies.

"I'm making more of my peanut-butter cookies," Bess told Nancy and George as she scooped peanut butter from a jar.

"I'm making white chocolate–chip cookies," George said. She shook a bag of white chocolate chips into a bowl.

"And I'm making oatmeal-raisin cookies," Nancy said.

Nancy measured out a cup of raisins in a measuring cup. Then she frowned. "Our parents will be here in an hour," she whispered to George and Bess. "And we still haven't solved the mystery!"

"We've got to be detectives *and* dessert chefs at the same time!" Bess whispered back. She glanced at the clock on the wall. "Fifty-nine minutes to go! We need a plan."

"A plan, a plan." Nancy peered around the kitchen. She drummed her fingertips on the countertop.

Just then, Kenny Bruder walked by. He reached into George's mixing bowl and grabbed a fistful of white chocolate chips. "What are these, candy?" he said.

"They're white chocolate chips. Give them back!" George cried out.

Kenny threw the chips back into the mixing bowl. "Yuck, no thanks! I'm allergic to chocolate."

Nancy, George, and Bess all stared at

each other. "Allergic to chocolate?" Nancy repeated.

"Yeah. It makes me break out in a rash. So what?" Kenny shrugged.

"But there's chocolate all *over* the place," Bess said, glancing around the kitchen.

"Monsieur Jadot knows I can't eat it. My mom made him promise I could make desserts without chocolate in it." Kenny shrugged again and kept walking.

Nancy saw him reach into Alison's mixing bowl and grab a handful of blueberries. "Hey!" Alison protested.

"He's allergic to chocolate! That means he *couldn't* have been the one with the chocolate fingerprints," Bess said after he'd gone.

Nancy nodded. "You're right! That only leaves three suspects: Brenda, Midori, and Annabelle."

And then something occurred to Nancy. "Hey, you know what, guys? There's only one student in this room whose desserts haven't gotten messed up."

George looked thoughtful. "Hmm, let's see. My cupcakes got messed up. Nancy's smoothie got messed up. Brenda, Alison, Kenny, and Jason got their butterscotch brownies messed up. And Bess's recipe got stolen."

"That leaves . . . Midori!" Bess gasped.

"I think she's the one," Nancy said, nodding. "There's just too much evidence against her, like the sparkly pink toothpaste."

"Plus I think she was making a chocolatey dessert yesterday," George added in a low voice. "It was chocolate mousse or something like that."

Nancy stared at Midori. She was across the kitchen, looking busy as she cracked eggs into a bowl.

"I think I have a plan," Nancy announced to Bess and George.

"What are you three up to? Why are you not baking cookies?"

Nancy's head shot up. Monsieur Jadot was standing there, his hands on his hips.

"Oh, we were just talking about . . . how to make our cookies yummier," Nancy fibbed.

"Annabelle and I have to go into the

supply closet for more ingredients. When we get back, I'd better see you hard at work," Monsieur Jadot told the girls.

"Yes, sir," Nancy said with a small salute.

She waited until Monsieur Jadot and Annabelle walked out the door. Then she turned to Bess and George.

"Guess what Monsieur Jadot told me? Oatmeal-raisin cookies are his favorite!" Nancy said in a loud voice.

Bess and George stared at Nancy. "Huh?" Bess said, confused. "What are you—"

"I'm sure my cookies will put me in first place for the Top Chef contest!" Nancy interrupted in an even louder voice.

Bess's eyes grew wide. "Oh . . . yeah . . . definitely," she said, nodding slowly.

"Way to go, Nancy!" George said.

Nancy looked around. Midori seemed to be listening. Actually, *everyone* in the room seemed to be listening.

"Okay," Nancy whispered to Bess and George. "Let's all go to the sink and wash our hands now."

"Huh?" George whispered back.

"It's part of my plan," Nancy explained. "I

just let Midori know that Monsieur Jadot loves oatmeal-raisin cookies."

"How do you know Monsieur Jadot loves oatmeal-raisin cookies?" Bess asked her.

"I don't. I just made that up. *Anyway,*" Nancy went on. "If we leave my bowl alone for a minute, Midori might be tempted to come over and dump salt in it or something. Then we can catch her in the act."

"Awesome!" George said enthusiastically.

Nancy, George, and Bess walked over to the big sink and began washing their hands. Nancy glanced over her shoulder.

Midori was approaching Nancy's workstation. She was carrying a small bottle in her hand.

*This is it!* Nancy thought.

# 8

# The Culprit Confesses

Nancy's heart was racing. Any second now, Midori would stop at Nancy's workstation and dump something nasty into her oatmeal raisin cookie batter!

But Midori kept walking. She handed the bottle to Alison. "Here, I'm done with the vanilla," Midori said.

"Huh? Oh, thanks," Alison said.

Midori and Alison continued talking for a moment. Nancy was confused. Why didn't Midori try to put something in Nancy's bowl?

And then Nancy saw a hand, then an arm, creeping up and over her workstation. The hand was holding a tiny vial.

*Someone's hiding behind my workstation!* Nancy realized.

Without wasting another second, Nancy ran over to her workstation. She peeked around the corner to see whose hand it was. At the same time, she grabbed the person's hand—hard.

*"Heeeeey!"*

The person stood up.

It was Jared Stein!

"Let go of my hand!" Jared complained.

Nancy glanced into her bowl of oatmeal raisin cookie–batter. Jared had squeezed a few drops of blue food coloring into it.

"You're the one who's been messing up everyone's recipes!" Nancy said angrily.

Jared looked around the room. Everyone was staring at him—including Midori. She looked really upset.

Jared frowned when he saw Midori's face. "Can I talk to you and George and Bess? In private?" he whispered to Nancy.

Nancy nodded. "Sure. But you're going to have to talk to Monsieur Jadot when he comes back."

"I know, I know."

Jared led Nancy, George, and Bess out into the hallway. It was empty.

Jared adjusted his glasses. He cleared his throat. Nancy could tell that he felt really badly.

"I know what I did was wrong," Jared said finally. "The thing is—I wanted Midori to win the contest!"

"*What?*" Nancy, Bess, and George said in unison.

"She never wins anything," Jared continued. "And I always win everything. Just once I wanted *her* to win. She's my best friend."

"So you decided to put pink toothpaste on my cupcakes?" George demanded.

"I kind of borrowed a tube of toothpaste from Midori's backpack," Jason admitted sheepishly.

"And you put baking soda and detergent in my strawberry-pineapple smoothie?" Nancy said.

Jason nodded. "I learned that trick in science class. But I only used a tiny bit of detergent! I didn't want you to get sick, in case you accidentally tasted the smoothie."

"And you stole page two of my grandma's peanut butter cookie-recipe?" Bess piped up.

"Yeah. I accidentally got chocolate all over it, though. I was making a chocolate smoothie that day. So I thought I'd put it in Kenny's backpack and make him look like the guilty one," Jared said.

"What about the salt in the butterscotch brownies?" Nancy asked him.

Jared shrugged. "Easy. I got to class early that day, and I put a bunch of salt in one of the sugar jars. I made sure Midori used the other one." He added, "I put salt in *my* brownies on purpose, so Midori's brownies would be the best."

"More shenanigans! *Now* what is going on?"

Monsieur Jadot and Annabelle were coming out of the classroom. Monsieur Jadot didn't look happy to see Nancy, George, Bess, and Jared standing out in the hallway.

"Jared has something to tell you," Nancy told Monsieur Jadot.

"Nancy's right," Jared said.

Nancy, Bess, and George exchanged a glance. The mystery was finally solved!

An hour later, Monsieur Jadot's kitchen was filled with people. Parents gathered around and sampled the students' desserts.

"Blue oatmeal-raisin cookies! I didn't know they came in that color," Hannah said to Nancy.

"They don't. They just kind of turned out that way," Nancy said with a smile.

"They're very yummy, Pudding Pie," Mr. Drew praised her.

Brenda's father, Mr. Carlton, was there with a photographer from *Today's Times*. It was the biggest newspaper in River Heights, and Mr. Carlton was the publisher. The photographer was taking pictures of all the kids in the classroom.

Nancy noticed that Jared and Midori were talking quietly in the corner. After confessing to Monsieur Jadot, Jared had apologized to everyone in the class about what he had done. Then Monsieur Jadot had announced that Jared would be washing all the dishes and pans today. That was his punishment for messing up everyone's recipes.

Nancy spooned some yummy-looking red punch from the punch bowl. It had cherries, orange slices, and real flowers floating in it. "Thanks for letting me take this class, Daddy," she told her father. "I learned all about making desserts. And I got to solve a mystery, too!"

"Which do you like better—being a dessert chef or a detective?" Mr. Drew asked her.

"Both!" Nancy said, giggling.

Just then Monsieur Jadot clinked a spoon against a glass. "Ladies and gentlemen!" he called out in a loud voice. The room fell silent. "Thank you all for being here today! As you know, this is the last day of our dessert-making class. Your children have been wonderful students as you can tell from tasting their creations."

The parents began clapping. Nancy, George, Bess, and the other kids clapped too.

"And thank you to my daughter, Annabelle, for being such a capable assistant!" Monsieur Jadot said, blowing a kiss to his daughter.

Annabelle, who was standing in the corner,

looked totally surprised. She blushed and smiled. Everyone clapped for her.

"One final thing!" Monsieur Jadot went on. "I would like to announce the winner of the Top Chef contest. Of course everyone here should win that prize. You all worked very hard. But I have finally made my decision. The winner is . . ."

Monsieur Jadot paused and waved a hand in Nancy's direction. "Mademoiselle Nancy Drew!"

"Yay!" Bess said, jumping up and down. George began jumping up and down too.

Everyone clapped and cheered. Nancy couldn't believe it. She had won the contest!

"See, Nancy! You're an awesome dessert chef *and* an awesome detective," George said, hugging Nancy.

"Totally!" Bess agreed. She hugged Nancy too.

Monsieur Jadot handed Nancy a small silver trophy. It read: TOP CHEF.

"Of course there is an even more excellent prize to come," Monsieur Jadot told her. "My special strawberry mousse cake! Just let me know when you want it, and I will deliver it personally to your house! One taste, and you will feel like you are in Paris!"

"Thank you, Monsieur Jadot!" Nancy said happily. She couldn't wait!

A few days later, Nancy sat down at her desk. She gazed up at her silver trophy, which she had put on top of her bookshelf, next to some of her favorite books. Then she took out her blue notebook and wrote:

Sometimes you'll do anything to make your best friend happy. You'll even do things that might make other people really miserable!

That's what Jared did by messing up everyone's desserts. But in the end he realized that he'd made a big mistake and he apologized.

Today I invited everyone from my class to come over to eat some of Monsieur Jadot's special strawberry mousse cake.

The cake was super-awesome! We ate the whole thing! And Monsieur Jadot was right—the cake made us feel like we were in Paris, France. He'd decorated the top of the cake with a French flag. The flag was made out of strawberries, blueberries, and whipped cream—yum!

I'm glad the mystery of the messed-up recipes has such a sweet ending!

Case closed.